VIOLET

A Very Special Hippo!

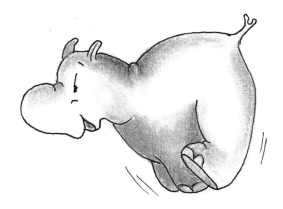

For Beth

Sibling Press
Level 2, Titchfield House
69/85 Tabernacle Street
London
EC2A 4RR

www.sibling-press.com

First Edition 2009

British Library in Cataloguing in Publication Data
A catalogue record for this book is available from the British Library

ISBN: 978-1-906847-37-1

Design by Ian Hughes, www.mousematdesign.com

Printed by Printer Trento, Italy

VIOLET

A Very Special Hippo!

Annie Taylor

CHAPTER 1

Violet

It was very quiet in the heat of the African noonday sun. All the animals had eaten their lunch and were putting their feet up in the shade. Even the smaller creatures were taking time off from being frightened because anyone who was likely to gobble them up was having a snooze.

Albert was snoozing too. Albert was a large, grey hippopotamus and a big snoozer. Unfortunately he was also a big snorer and his snoring could be heard for miles around. Snoozing and snoring were what Albert liked to do best – except on Sundays or special occasions when he liked to cool down with a nice wallow in the mud. While he was snoozing, his lovely wife Mavis, a sublimely happy hippo, was pottering about and humming a little tune to herself.

She was a little preoccupied with her thoughts, wondering where her life was going and what was the true nature of the universe, so she wasn't really paying attention to where she was putting her feet. Suddenly she tripped over and fell SMACK on her nose with a resounding PLONK.

'OUCH!' squeaked a small voice. 'Look where you're going!'

Mavis sat up and looked around her, but she couldn't see where the voice was coming from.

'Who's that?' she said.

'It's me,' said the voice.

Mavis looked down and there, right under her nose, partly hidden by the grass, was the smallest hippopotamus she had ever seen.

'How do you do?' said the tiny creature.

'How do you do?' said Mavis, feeling slightly unnerved.
'What's your name?' she added, remembering her manners.

'Violet,' replied the little hippo. 'I've come to live with you.'

'Oh!' said Mavis, feeling more confused than ever. 'I'm afraid
I'll have to ask my husband about that,' she said, trying to
sound a little stern. 'It seems a bit irregular.'

'Oh no, not really, I need somewhere to live and there's plenty
of room here,' said Violet.

'Oh my goodness,' thought Mavis, and then she thought,
'What am I going to do with her?' and then, 'What ever will
Albert say?', and finally, 'Oh, but she is *very* sweet!', and then,
aloud, she said rather briskly, 'We'd better go and find Albert.'

'What's all this? What's all this?' asked a gruff voice and there
was Albert who had just woken up from his snooze.

'Oh hello dear, I was just coming to find you,' said Mavis
rather breathlessly. 'We, um . . . well . . . we have a . . . visitor
. . . Actually, she says she's come to live with us!'

'She's WHAT?' said Albert staring at the diminutive hippo.

Mavis, summoning a little more confidence now, repeated what she had just told him.

Albert sat down with a bump. He scratched his ear and then, because he really couldn't think of anything else to say, he exclaimed, 'BUT she's far too SMALL!'

Violet decided to ignore this and reminded him instead that all the best things come in little packages, and then she proceeded to look very 'moved in' indeed.

Mavis was a kindly soul and never one to upset another's feelings, so she thought there would be no harm in letting Violet stay for a while, at least until she'd had time to work out what on earth they ought to do about her.

Albert continued sitting where he was, looking slightly cross and more than a little puzzled. He wondered whether he should perhaps stomp up and down a bit just to demonstrate who was boss around here. But then it was very hot and it seemed a little too exhausting to do all that, so he gave up.

And that's how Violet came to live with Albert and Mavis.

CHAPTER 2

Life was Nearly Perfect

Mavis soon got used to having little Violet around and she was very careful not to tread on her again. Violet definitely filled a gap she had noticed in her life and everything would have been just perfect had it not been for the fact that some of the other animals were not very nice to Violet. Because she was a bit smaller than your average hippo, they teased her and started to call her 'the shrinking Violet'.

These rather rude animals had simply forgotten what it was like to be small. To give you an idea, a hyena, coming across her for the first time, laughed so hysterically that he got the hiccups. A snake hissed himself into a horrible giggling knot and stuck that way for a week, and an elephant and his family hooted and trumpeted so much when they saw Violet that they all developed terribly sore trunks and had to wrap them up in banana skins to make them better.

Mavis could see that this upset Violet, so she decided to try some of Great Aunt Gertrude's remedies for making things grow. She spent days searching for mysterious herbs, but they only put Violet to sleep and didn't make a scrap of difference.

Fortunately, it seemed that the younger animals were not the least bit concerned about Violet's size. One day, some of them called by to ask if she could come out to play and Violet, who had been sitting around in a bit of a daydream, jumped up eagerly and Mavis, who was really pleased at this turn of events, said 'Off you go, but be careful and don't wander too far from home.'

CHAPTER 3

Something Odd About Violet

All the little animals had a lovely time playing games of chase and hide-and-seek and Violet had soon made friends with everyone. But, as is often the way, no sooner had things begun to go smoothly, than something happened to upset the applecart.

They had strayed a long way from home and were much too close to the jungle where dangerous things can happen, when quite suddenly a young zebra let out a shriek 'Eeeek . . . look at Violet!' he cried.

Everyone gasped. Right before their eyes, Violet was turning PINK! First the tip of her nose began to turn pink, then her toes, and before you could say Wally the Warthog, she was just about PINK all over!

Naturally everyone thought that this was a huge joke and they all fell about laughing. But Violet didn't seem to hear, she was staring directly ahead and shaking like a little pink jelly.

Then as suddenly as the laughter had started it stopped. The youngsters all sat bolt upright and pricked up their ears. A little way off they could hear a noise . . . swish, swoosh, snap, swish swoosh, snap. It was coming closer, swish, swoosh, snap . . .

Then Wally the Warthog's fifteenth cousin twice removed remembered the stories his mum had told him about playing near the edge of the jungle:

'It's a CROCODILE!' he gasped and with that they all turned tail and. squealing noisily, they bolted off in the direction of home. But Violet remained rooted to the spot, glowing pinkly.

'SNAP, CRUNCH, SCHLURP, DRIBBLE, . . . YUM, YUM!' rumbled a very nasty voice close behind her. 'I smell a scrumptious young hippo!' and out of the jungle crawled the largest, ugliest crocodile you can possibly imagine. He was dribbling from one corner of his mouth and grinding his great yellow teeth together.

Then suddenly the crocodile
went very quiet and in
the horrible silence that
followed it looked as though Violet's
days were numbered.

He was holding his smelly breath
and inching closer to her tail. His huge
jaws began to open, he licked his lips . . .
in just one gulp it would be 'Goodbye,
Violet'.

But that would be the end of this story. Instead, there was a
loud BANG! as a gun was fired. Even ferocious crocodiles
don't like guns and he quickly scuttled away. Poor Violet was
startled out of her trance. Head down, she started running for
home as fast as her little legs could carry her. She ran so fast
that she ran straight into the legs of the man with the gun
and bowled him over.

When they got home the other little animals panted out the
whole story. When their parents heard about Violet, they said
their children had been so busy watching her turn pink they
had not noticed the crocodile and told them never to play
with Violet again.

Meanwhile back in the jungle the man with the gun sat by his campfire dreaming about how rich and famous he was going to be when he captured the world's only miniature pink hippopotamus.

CHAPTER 4

And Then IT Happened Again

When Violet got home Mavis asked her what had happened.

'Well,' said Violet, 'I'm not sure. I heard something that sounded dangerous and I wanted to warn the others, but I couldn't move. I saw the tip of my nose was changing colour, but after that I really didn't know anything until there was a loud bang and I woke up and saw the crocodile running away.'

'Hurumph,' said Mavis. She had heard about the pink 'thing' from a mum who had been round to the mud hole to complain to her, so she said: 'Sounds like you saved their little skins if you ask me. There's gratitude for you.'

Over the next few days Violet tried to ignore the other animals making fun of her, but it wasn't very easy – even the young ones thought she was odd now. Then one morning, Mavis decided that Violet needed a change of scenery and after breakfast she announced that they were all going on a picnic.

'Don't like picnics,' grumbled Albert. But Mavis took no notice and when she had packed up a basket they all set off. The picnic spot was in a clearing on the very edge of the jungle but Violet felt quite safe going there this time with Albert and Mavis. Mavis unloaded the picnic basket and laid out a lovely spread of grass cakes and grass biscuits and Aunt Mabel's very special Mud Hole Surprise for pudding.

After the picnic, Violet was chasing a butterfly and Albert was looking for a suitable place to have a ziz, when quite suddenly IT happened again. Mavis looked up to make sure that Violet was all right and saw her standing stock-still quivering from head to toe and, yes, she was gradually turning PINK!

Mavis's jaw dropped open in amazement. Albert hadn't noticed anything at all as he was busy sorting out a nest for his after-lunch snooze. He was pushing bits of grass and leaves into a nice comfortable bed, when suddenly, snap, crash, thud and a huge net came down out of the tree he was rummaging under, narrowly missing his nose and landing very close to Violet.

'Phew! That was close,' spluttered Albert and then, turning round to see where the others were, he gasped as he caught sight of the bright pink hippo behind him. 'What's all this?' he rumbled, at which point, the pink began to disappear and Violet stirred. 'Oh Albert, thank goodness, you're quite safe,' she said.

A man with a gun was hiding behind a tree and when he saw his net falling down and missing Violet, he muttered a curse under his breath.

CHAPTER 5

A Royal Command

After the picnic, life went on much as before at the mud hole without any strange 'pink' happenings, until one morning a message came from the King of the Beasts commanding all animals to attend a very important meeting in the jungle.

Albert was disgruntled: more travelling! He stomped up and down feeling cross. Violet who liked adventure, jumped up and down feeling excited. Mavis liked to be organised so she bustled to and fro packing grass cakes for the journey.

And when the stomping and jumping and to-ing and fro-ing was done, they all set off.

They plodded along for miles, Violet riding on Albert's back. By the time they arrived at the edge of the jungle they had been joined by all sorts of creatures. There were zebras, giraffes, hyenas, snakes, giant elephants and tiny mice, all hurrying and scurrying along, chattering excitedly,

At last they came to a clearing where a huge crowd was already gathered. All the animals were sitting in rows, everyone talking at once and no one listening. Violet could feel the excitement mounting. Suddenly, there was a hush as three monkey sentries marched into the clearing:

'Make way for His Majesty!' they cried. Then they blew a fanfare of raspberries and into the clearing prowled the most magnificent lion you could possibly imagine – His Majesty, the King of the Beasts. On His Majesty's back rode a tiny mouse, carrying a huge banana leaf to shade His Royal Highness from the sun. Behind him came a procession of the palace guard and then the Queens

and their ladies-in-waiting. Everyone cheered.

When the last of the troops had marched to their posts, the King's High Chamberlain, a very elderly vulture, announced that His Majesty would now speak. The King cleared his throat.

'Now the court will hear all the grumbles and then we will get down to the business of the meeting.'

There was a very long list of grumbles to get through. There was a monkey accused of stealing a rhino's horn; a snake complained that someone had stolen his skin; on and on and on it went. Violet soon got bored and decided to go exploring. She slipped down off Albert's back and tiptoed away.

CHAPTER 6

Fire!

Neither Mavis nor Albert noticed Violet go. Albert was snoozing and Mavis was listening to a fascinating case about an elephant whose sleep was being disturbed by a mouse building a nest in his trunk. Just as the King was about to pass sentence on the poor unfortunate mouse (a distant relative of the one who carried his banana leaf), someone let out a great bellow of laughter. 'Look at that!' they shouted and all the animals turned to see what was happening.

'Oh no, look!' gasped Mavis prodding Albert, for there, standing on an ant heap just outside the circle, was Violet and she was bright PINK.

 All the animals had turned to look. There were shrieks and whistles, all sorts of rude noises and howls of laughter.

But Violet didn't hear a thing. She was staring straight ahead

at the King and getting pinker and pinker. The King let out a great ROAR and silence fell. He began to stalk towards Violet, and he looked very CROSS indeed!

'What is the meaning of this?' he growled. 'Who said you could turn pink without my permission?' Violet went on quivering silently and the King was furious. He opened his mouth to let out another roar, but he suddenly froze, he sniffed, his mane stood on end and then he spun round to the crowd.

'FIRE!' he roared. 'I CAN SMELL FIRE! GET EVERYONE OUT OF HERE! FIRE!' And with that he turned on his heel and in a shake of a whisker, sped off down the jungle path with his personal bodyguard swinging through the trees above his head.

It was chaos. Animals rushed about in every direction, tripped over each other, shouted, roared, squeaked, pushed and shoved . . . And all the while, the fire was getting closer and they could feel the heat and see the great flames licking up into the sky as trees crashed to the ground.

CHAPTER 7

Reggie Rhino

Eventually everyone ran in the right direction including Mavis and Albert who were calling to Violet as they went. But Violet didn't hear them and again this might have been the end of our story if it wasn't for a very thoughtful rhino called Reggie.

While everyone was dashing about yelling 'Fire!' Reggie was putting two and two together. HE knew that hippos don't normally turn pink and that this could have something to do with the fire. He tiptoed up to the little pink hippo and said quietly, 'Ahem, excuse me, my dear I think we're in a spot of bother.'

'Um?' said Violet, slowly coming out of her trance.

'You see,' said Reggie, 'the jungle's on fire so perhaps you should hop on my back so that we can get away!'

'Oh good gracious!' squeaked Violet, her eyes opening wide in dismay. All around them the flames were dancing nearer and nearer. Without further ado she jumped onto Reggie's back and away they went. The flames were so close that they singed Reggie's tail. He was quite frightened so, as he ran, he puffed out a little song to make himself feel braver:

I'm Reggie the Rhino don't you know

That's R-H-I-N-O

I'm brave and I'm strong

And before very long

We will be safe ho . . . ho . . . !

Reggie ran so fast that before long the fire was just a whiff of smoke behind them. Eventually he stopped and Violet slipped to the ground. As soon as Reggie had got his breath back, he said, 'Now young hippo, suppose you just tell me about this pink trick of yours!'

Violet sniffed, took a deep breath and tried to explain.

'Well, I think there *is* something significant about this pinkification,' she said. ' I seem to be the first to sense danger. The trouble is that I want to shout a warning, but instead I don't seem able to move and then I start to change colour.'

'Ah . . . "Pinkification",' repeated Reggie who liked long words.

'First my knees get wobbly, and then I feel as though I'm floating. I get warmer and I can see my nose start to turn pink.' Violet began to sob. Reggie noticed that the tears trickling down her nose were like great pink rose petals. He gave her a comforting nudge.

'There, there,' he said, 'Stiff nostrils and all that! Someone should hear about this useful talent of yours and just how brave you are. I think we should tell the King!'

'Oh no,' cried Violet, 'I'd be much too embarrassed. Anyway, I really must be trotting home now.' So saying, she picked herself up and was about to set off, but it was getting dark and Reggie wisely pointed out that it would be better to get a good night's sleep before setting out again. So they curled up in a convenient spot and soon fell fast asleep.

CHAPTER 8

Hippo-napped!

The next morning, Violet was feeling a lot brighter and Reggie said he would take her home. They walked and walked until the sun was high in the sky and to be quite honest they were just the teeniest bit lost.

They were about to stop for lunch, when they heard muffled voices in the distance. Soon they came into a clearing and there, in the middle, HM the King of the Beasts lay fast asleep. The little mouse was fanning him with a large leaf and nearby, his bodyguards were lying on their tummies, whispering to each other.

'I'd love to take a closer peep at him,' whispered Violet.

'Go on then,' said Reggie, 'I'll stay here, but be careful not to wake him.'

Violet began to creep forward on her tiptoes, but she stepped on a twig and suddenly stopped. One of the bodyguards, heard the twig snap and looked up.

''Ere, WOT do you think you're a DOIN' of?' he hissed, 'Don't you know the likes of you 'as no place in the presence of 'is Majesty when 'e's 'avin a kip?'

But Violet did not reply. First her nose started to glow, then her ears, and very soon she was turning pink all over. All the bodyguards started giggling.

Reggie, hearing the commotion, came out of his hiding place to be greeted by the sight of a bright pink Violet and the King still snoozing peacefully.

'Wake up his Majesty quickly – something terrible is about to happen!' he shouted.

'And 'oo the 'eck do you think you are?' demanded a guard, moving forward to stop Reggie in his tracks.

But Reggie ignored him and shouted at the top of his lungs, 'Wake up, Your Majesty!' But now the King started to snore.

The little mouse put down his leaf, and in spite of the nervous disposition he had inherited from his Uncle Wilfred, he made a mighty leap, grabbed the King's whiskers and began to swing on them for all he was worth. The King yawned, opened one royal eye very slowly and then the other. The little mouse jumped down quickly in case he suddenly became a tasty royal snack.

'Your Majesty, you're in terrible danger,' cried Reggie.

'Eh? What's going on –' began the King, but he never finished the sentence. Just when he caught sight of Violet, a bullet zipped past his ear.

'HUMAN!' they all screamed with one voice. Reggie shouted at Violet to follow them as they all galloped out of the clearing with bullets whistling past their whiskers.

But Violet could not follow them, for as the pink disappeared and she came out of her trance, the man with the gun came out from behind a bush. He crept up behind her and threw a great big sack over her head.

CHAPTER 9

The King Hears the Story

'Wow, what a terrible day!', puffed Reggie. 'Well done Violet,' he called over his shoulder. 'The King may not know it yet, but that's the second time you've saved his life.'

But there was silence behind him. Reggie spun round. No Violet.

'I was sure she was with us, I heard her,' he gasped. 'Violet, where are you?'

'What's wrong?' demanded the King, who had stopped when he heard Reggie cry out.

'It's Violet, sire, the little pink hippo,' said Reggie. 'She saved us all and now I think something terrible must have happened.' And with that he spilled the beans and told the King the whole story about Violet and why she turned pink.

'What a brave little hippo,' said the King. 'We must go back and find her.'

They retraced their footsteps to the clearing, but they were too late. The fate that was worse than crocodiles, worse even than jungle fires, had happened to Violet: she had been captured by a Hollywood film producer.

CHAPTER 10

What's Happened to Violet?

The film producer's name was Mr J. Arnold Schleppenberger Jr. What was he doing in Africa you may ask. Well, his wife, Mrs J. Arnold Schleppenberger Jr, had very expensive tastes and she had sent him to Africa to shoot a crocodile for her so that her favourite fashion designer could make her a handbag.

While he was hunting for crocodiles, J. Arnold was also racking his brains to find a BIG IDEA for a film, when quite by accident he stumbled across a group of young animals playing together. Then he saw one of them, an unusually small hippo, turn pink. Now, J. Arnold did not know much about animals, but he knew this was not what hippos normally did and when it came to sniffing out a good idea for a film, well, he was the man with a nose for it.

J. Arnold forgot all about the handbag hunt when he saw that ugly old crocodile was about to eat Violet. He just wanted to frighten the crocodile away with his gun and then capture the hippo. But as you know, Violet ran away. After that, J. Arnold looked everywhere for her but he couldn't find her.

His luck changed, however, when he came across Violet in the clearing with the King. Having frightened all the other animals away, he rushed up to the hippo and popped a sack over her head.

'Got you!' he cried. And with that he slung her over his shoulder and carried her off.

So when Reggie and the King finally reached the clearing they were too late to save Violet. Luckily a little bird had witnessed everything and told them what had happened.

'Oh dear me,' groaned Reggie, 'I've let her down.' And there and then he made up his mind to rescue Violet.

CHAPTER 11

Violet Flies First Class

 'Two tickets for Hollywood please,' said Mr J. Arnold Schleppenberger Jr to the ticket man at the airport.

'Yes, sir,' said the man behind the ticket counter at the airport who thought he recognised someone famous. 'Where is the other passenger, sir?'

'Here she is,' said J Arnold, 'My latest discovery – Miss Eudora. Take a good look at a bright new star of stage and screen.'

The ticket man looked up from his computer terminal and seeing no-one there, leaned forward and peered over the edge of the counter. There sat Violet, on the end of a diamond-studded lead, the tiniest hippopotamus he had ever seen.

'But you can't take THAT on board, sir!' stammered the unfortunate man.

'Young man,' said Mr J. Arnold Schleppenberger Jr 'I am a

famous Hollywood film producer and I can do just about anything I like. Why you're looking at the greatest new star since Miss Piggy. Now hand over those tickets.'

Reluctantly, the ticket man did as he was told.

J. Arnold Schleppenberger Jr and Violet were soon seated in the first class section of a huge airplane. J. Arnold was very pleased with himself and he patted Violet affectionately as he sipped his drink.

Poor Violet was very tired and miserable. She was glad to be out of the sack, but she didn't like being on a lead. She didn't like being called 'Eudora' either, but when she tried to tell them what her name really was the humans didn't seem to understand 'hippopotish'. She wanted to go home; she missed Albert and Mavis, and she wondered where her new friend Reggie was.

Luckily for Violet, there were lots of children on the airplane. They kept peeping into the first class cabin and then tiptoeing in with sweets for her. The sweets tasted very nice, but the toffees stuck her teeth together.

CHAPTER 12

Hollywood

At last the airplane landed. At the airport J. Arnold and Violet were surrounded by a big crowd of excited reporters and photographers all asking Violet lots of silly questions:

'What's it like down there in ol' Africa, honey?'

'Have you known Mr Schleppenberger long?'

'Is this your first movie?'

 'Well, actually… ' Violet began, but then she remembered that no one could understand her and soon J. Arnold led her away, through the airport and out to a huge limousine.

'Where to, Mr S?' asked the chauffeur.

'The Beverly Hills Hilton,' drawled J. Arnold. 'I've booked Miss Eudora a suite.'

After a frightening journey weaving in and out of hundreds of cars, they pulled up outside a big hotel and a man in a uniform opened the car door. J. Arnold had to give Violet a shove to get her out of the car.

The hotel manager kept a very straight face when he was asked to book a hippopotamus into one of his best suites – after all this was Hollywood.

Violet's suite was very grand. There was an enormous bed, a huge TV and a bath that was almost as big as the mud hole.

When she was alone Violet decided to explore.

First she climbed onto the bed. 'Weeeeeeeee!' she giggled as she bounced up and down.

Then she accidentally sat on the remote control for the TV. 'OOOh!' she exclaimed as The Simpsons came onto the screen.

When she was tired of watching the TV Violet went to investigate the bathroom. She jumped up on the side to get a better look at the bath, knocking a pot plant into it.

Then 'Ouch!' she said as she sat on the tap.

The tap began to drip making a muddy puddle in the bottom of the bath. She slid into it with a plop.

'Ahhhh!' she said, splashing about in the mud. 'Now that's more like it!'

The bathroom was in a fine mess by the time she finally climbed out of the bath. And at last, tired out, she curled up on the floor and went to sleep.

CHAPTER 13

Reggie to the Rescue

Back in Africa, the King's spies brought news that Violet had been taken away in a big silver bird so the King held a meeting with his Council of the Elders. When they had finished they sent for Reggie the Rhino and gave him their advice.

'To find Violet,' they told him, 'you will have to set out immediately and make your way across the great watering hole.' (It was really the sea but none of them had ever been there.)

So Reggie packed a parcel of grass cakes and set off. He plodded on for days and days, talking to every animal, insect and bird he met, but there was no more news of Violet or the great silver bird.

At long last Reggie saw the great watering hole, shimmering in the sunlight. He sat down and unwrapped the last of his grass cakes. As he munched he thought and as he thought he worried. He was still munching and worrying, when a voice said, 'What's a rhinoceros doing so far from home?'

Reggie turned round and there stood four pelicans. Perhaps they could help; he knew they were well-travelled birds, so he told them the story. When he had finished, the oldest pelican, whose name was Orlando, said, 'Well, old chap, it's my guess they've taken your little friend to the land the humans call America. We go there on our holidays sometimes – in fact, I have family there. I well remember…' And with that off he rambled on a terribly long story, which Reggie politely tried to follow.

At length Orlando remembered Reggie's problem.

'Ahem, sorry, I digress,' he said. 'I think we may be able to help you.' Reggie held his breath as the pelican continued, 'You'll simply have to fly there!' he said.

Reggie looked aghast.

'Rhinos don't fly!' he exclaimed. But Orlando had a very good plan up his beak.

'We'll make you a nest you can travel in while we do the

flying,' he announced. Reggie thought this sounded a tiny bit worrying – after all a solid sort of chap liked to have all four feet on the ground.

The pelicans got weaving very quickly and pretty soon they had a nest made for Reggie. Reggie climbed in gingerly and lay on his tummy so that his front legs were over one end and his back legs were over the other. Then the pelicans took hold of the sides and told Reggie to shut his eyes and begin a countdown, 'Five, four, three, two, one . . . ohhhhhhh!' and with a huff and a puff and a mighty flutter of wings, they were airborne. It was a little wobbly at first, but when Reggie realised he was flying and seemed to be quite safe he shouted with glee, 'Look at me fly!'

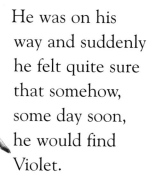

He was on his way and suddenly he felt quite sure that somehow, some day soon, he would find Violet.

CHAPTER 14

Violet Superstar?

Violet spent a restless night and was woken in the middle of a particularly frightening dream about fires by a loud knock at the door. In marched J. Arnold Schleppenberger Jr, followed by his secretary and an army of publicity people.

'Morning, Eudora,' he said. 'Today's your big day! Folks, meet Eudora.' Everyone said 'Hi'. 'Eudora I'm gonna make you into a great star of the big screen! You'll be famous all over the world.'

'But please sir,' Violet exclaimed, 'I don't want to be famous!' She had already known fame of a sort and she didn't like it much, but of course J. Arnold couldn't know that – he didn't speak hippopotish!

'Yes, yes, my dear,' he went on, lighting a big cigar that made her cough, 'I know how grateful you are! You wait 'til you see the part! It's a really great script the boys have come up with: laughs, thrills, a cast of thousands and you the star, silent and mysterious, the little pink heroine who just wants to be left alone.'

After that everyone was ready to go. They hustled Violet downstairs and out to another great big limousine to drive her to the 21st Century Schleppenberger Film Studios. As they drove through the gates, it was like entering another world: people rushing around all over the place, actors and actresses in funny costumes: monsters and Martians, cowboys and Indians.

Violet was taken to her dressing room to have her nose powdered. The dressing room had a big gold star on the door.

When she was ready, Violet was taken to the set to be introduced to the director.

Alfredo, the director, had worked all his life in the film industry. He had dealt with numerous temperamental stars of all shapes and sizes, but never before had his leading lady been a hippopotamus. Fortunately for Violet he'd had a nice cup of green tea before she arrived and he was feeling a bit calmer.

The first day's filming went by without too many problems. Violet was guided through each scene and when she got it right, someone gave her a sugar lump.

However there was one thing worrying Violet. She had found out that she was meant to turn pink – the director kept discussing it with the cameraman. But Violet knew she wasn't going to turn pink – she didn't feel frightened, just homesick.

And so, as the days went by and there was no sign of Violet changing colour, Alfredo was getting more and more agitated. At the end of the week J. Arnold paid them a visit and was told that his superstar just wasn't 'in the pink'.

Well, of course, J. Arnold was not a very happy little Schleppenberger. A conference was called and it was decided that they would continue filming for just one more day before taking drastic action. They would leave the 'pink' scenes until the end of the day and then, if Violet still hadn't changed colour, the man from the props department would have to paint her pink!

CHAPTER 15

Reggie on the High Seas

Reggie's first flight was going well. The pelicans were covering great distances, occasionally touching down on small islands to rest and catch fish and although Reggie was enjoying his bird's-eye view, he was grateful for these breaks when he could put four feet down on solid ground for a while.

One day when they were resting, Orlando Pelican said to him, 'Reggie old fellow, the time has come for us to part company. We're going to fly on to a place called Florida, but my hunch is that you need to go to Hollywood. America is a very big place, you see.'

'Oh dear!' said Reggie, 'what shall I do now?'

'I've been thinking about that,' said Orlando. 'There are some dolphins who live near here. I think I'll pay them a visit and see if we can arrange something for you.'

Orlando found the dolphins at school. They were practising high jump in the sea. It turned out that their teacher Pythagoras was an old chum of his, so he asked him to come and have a chat with Reggie.

Pythagoras was very old and wise, had travelled all over the world and had been to America on his holidays. So when he heard about Violet he was sure Orlando was right and that the humans had taken her to Hollywood.

'In fact,' he said, 'I'd like to go to America again and I think my youngsters would benefit from some long-distance swimming practice – so we'll guide you there.'

Reggie was beginning to feel despondent. He hoped they weren't going to ask him to swim and he secretly wished he was back home in Africa basking in the sun.

'You're also going to need an interpreter in case you have to negotiate with these humans,' Pythagoras continued, wrinkling his forehead. 'My old friend Mynah in London talks a bit of "human". I'll send word to him. Now if you'd like to say goodbye to Orlando and his friends, we should be going.'

And with that six cheerful dolphins appeared around a rock pulling behind them an enormous shell.

'We borrowed this from a friend,' they called. 'Jump in!'

Reggie, relieved that he wouldn't have to swim, climbed in carefully and sat down. Then the dolphins whisked him away across the tops of the waves, the spray splashing his nose. It was fun and he soon got his sea legs. Above, the pelicans called to him and he looked up to see them looping the loop over his head - they looked so funny he nearly fell out of the shell laughing.

'Good luck, Reggie!' they called. 'We'll look out for you on the way home. Good luck . . . good luck . . . '

CHAPTER 16

The Gull Brings News

The dolphins were always laughing and joking and even Pythagoras, who was quite strict, usually had a twinkle in his eye. They journeyed on for several days until one morning the coast of America came into view and a seagull appeared with the first proper news of Violet. The gull perched on the side of the shell.

'Your friend has been spotted in Hollywood,' he told Reggie. 'The birds there tell me they have seen her being taken each day to a big building. They said it may be difficult to rescue her as she is never alone.'

Reggie frowned. All he had thought about on this journey was finding Violet. He'd never planned how he was going to rescue her when he did find her. He couldn't even speak the language so he couldn't persuade the humans to let her go.

Then they heard a great squawking overhead. Looking up,

Reggie saw a very odd sight: a thoroughly bedraggled-looking bird in a hat and waistcoat was flying in an alarmingly wobbly manner straight towards him.

'It's Mynah,' shouted the young dolphins, and indeed it was. The gulls had found him on his way to a fishing holiday in Bognor Regis. He was not best pleased at the idea of abandoning his holiday, but when they told him the whole story, he decided it could just be the break into show business he'd been looking for.

Now in a great kerfuffle of feathers and with a rather undignified landing technique, Mynah perched on the edge of the shell and offered a bedraggled wing tip to Reggie.

'How de do?' he said. 'Mynah translations at your service. Do I hear on the bird line that you're in a spot of bother?' And being a bit of a show off he began counting backwards from five hundred which impressed Reggie no end.

CHAPTER 17

Pink Paint!

It was dusk when the dolphins finally put Reggie and Mynah ashore on a deserted sandy beach. Having all four feet back on the ground Reggie completely forgot his mission. He gambolled about on the sand, splashed in and out of the waves, rolled, turned somersaults, found a shallow pool and rolled some more.

Finally, Mynah said they should go. He perched himself on Reggie's back and they set off towards Hollywood, saying goodbye to the dolphins who said they would wait in case they could help Reggie and Violet get home.

Mynah was rather a noisy travelling companion who never stopped talking, but they made good progress and later that night they went to sleep right under a giant sign that said 'Hollywood'.

Perhaps it was because the people who live in Hollywood are used to seeing some very odd sights, or perhaps it was because they were just too busy to notice, but the next morning a rhino wandering along the street with a mynah bird on his back failed to attract much attention. A policeman stopped them once, but Mynah simply said, 'It's all right, Ossifer, this 'ere rhino's wiv me.' The policeman was so taken aback at hearing the bird speak that he forgot to arrest them.

When they reached the great gates of the 21st Century Schleppenberger Film Studios, they just marched through as

though they had been going there every day. Mynah asked a man if he had seen a small hippo anywhere and they were directed to the stage where Violet was filming. They tiptoed inside.

Reggie couldn't believe his eyes. Violet was on the set, looking as unhappy as a hippo could be. There were bright lights everywhere, all shining on Violet. A make-up lady was dabbing powder on Violet's nose and another was trying to  straighten Violet's little tail. Cameras pointed at her, microphones hung above her. Worst of all, in front of her stood Alfredo and J. Arnold and a man with a big pot of pink paint. And they were all very angry.

CHAPTER 18

Saved by the Bird

'This is your big scene, Eudora! This is where you save the day! This is where you become a star! This is where YOU'RE SUPPOSED TO TURN PINK!' yelled J. Arnold.

Violet hung her head. She tried to turn pink. She tried as hard as she ever could. She held her breath but she just turned blue. She thought of eating snails but she just turned green. She thought of J. Arnold in his underpants but she just turned red. She couldn't think of anything to make her turn pink.

'Motivation!' yelled Alfredo. 'You have to feel pink to be pink!'

'Think pink thoughts,' pleaded J. Arnold.

'Pretend you're candyfloss,' said Alfredo.

'Pretend you're a pink flamingo,' begged J. Arnold.

'Pretend you're Barbara Cartland,' said Alfredo.

It was no good. No matter what she pretended to be or what she thought, Violet just couldn't turn pink. Then Alfredo ordered the props man to bring in everything he could think of that was pink.

They brought in a pretty pink rose.

They brought in a shiny pink Cadillac.

They brought in lots of cupcakes with bright pink icing.

They brought in pink lemonade.

Nothing worked. Poor Violet grew more and more miserable. The lights made her hot, her ears were sore from all the yelling and she had a headache from all the thinking. Watching his friend become more and more miserable was too much for Reggie.

Reggie charged onto the set, Mynah balancing on his back.

'Violet!' cried the rhino.

The sight of Reggie charging towards her made Violet blink to see whether she was dreaming. She ran to greet him.

'Reggie, is that really you?' she cried.

She gave Reggie a big kiss, which left him quite discombobulated, but he did his best to look fiercely over her shoulder at the bewildered film men.

'See here,' fumed J. Arnold. 'Who are you? Why are you interrupting my picture? Why are you distracting my star? Can't you see we're TRYING TO DO PINK HERE?'

'"Mynah, talk to them,' said Reggie. 'Tell them they're doing it all wrong!'

Mynah cleared his throat, puffed out his feathers, thrust his beak out at J. Arnold, and, in his best imitation of an American gangster, said, 'You listen up, bud, you listen up real good. That ol' hippo ain't never done you no 'arm. You make with all dat pink stuff to put her in the pink and instead you give poor Violet a pink fit! Petri-fying a little hippo ain't gonna bring home the bacon or your movie in on schedule. You dirty rats! It takes brains to fix dis, not muscle! You wanna work in dis town again then listen up!'

J. Arnold and Alfredo were shocked. No one had ever talked to them like that before. But Mynah sounded very much like a bird it didn't pay to argue with. They nodded. 'We're listening,' they said at the same time.

'OK, OK, I might just be able to help you, for a small consideration. Let me introduce you to my pal, Reg the Rhino.'

Reggie nodded, his horn coming very close to J. Arnold's nose. 'Mynah,' he said, 'first, you tell Mr Schleppenberger that if he will promise that Violet can come home with me afterwards, I think I can help him finish his film.'

Mynah told J. Arnold and Alfredo Reggie's condition for helping. To tell the truth, J. Arnold and Alfredo agreed with a certain amount of relief. Working with a very small hippo brought very big problems.

'Good,' said Reggie. 'Violet, why don't you go sit down?' When Violet had gone, Reggie whispered to Mynah, 'OK, now this is what we have to do . . . '

CHAPTER 19

Crocodile!

 'Places, everyone!' yelled Alfredo, through the large megaphone he always used when directing.

The make-up lady powdered Violet's nose again and the make-up lady's assistant put a bit more polish on Violet's toes.

'Lights!' yelled Alfredo and all the lights went on and the make-up ladies scurried from the set.

'Camera!' yelled Alfredo and everyone went quiet.

'ACTION!' yelled Alfredo – and nothing happened.

Violet stood, thinking all the pink thoughts she could, as hard as possible. Then all of a sudden, Violet felt her skin tingle. A shiver ran right up her back and her body went still and stiff. She felt the warm glow of pink spreading right through her.

'Yum yum, scrumptious,' she heard someone mutter behind her.

Coming closer and closer was a large, wrinkly, ugly crocodile, gobbling up a trail of food with its long, snapping jaws. First, there was a packet of salt and vinegar crisps. CRUNCH! went the jaws. 'Lovely,' drooled the crocodile. Then there was a cheese and pickle sandwich. CHOMP! went the jaws. 'Delicious,' dribbled the crocodile. Smelly, grungy, green saliva began to drip from the crocodile's mouth as he mashed the sandwich with his sharp yellow teeth. SNAP! went the jaws as the crocodile scoffed a pink cupcake and took a step closer to another pink cupcake – and to Violet.

Violet quivered. The crocodile was coming straight towards her. She couldn't move. She watched it open its huge mouth again, a trail of disgusting saliva dripping from its teeth. She felt herself grow pinker and pinker as she realised that the trail of pink cupcakes led straight to her!

CLACK! went the jaws. 'BEEE-YOUTIFUL!' burped the crocodile as he swallowed the last cupcake. He sniffed. And then he sniffed again. 'MMMMM, my favourite! Plumptious-scrumptious young hippo!' And he opened his mouth as wide as could be and took another step closer to Violet.

'OOOMPH!' said the crocodile as Reggie landed right on his back. And the last thing the crocodile remembered before fainting was the sight of the brightest, pinkest hippopotamus ever seen.

'Cut!' yelled Alfredo.

'Wonderful, wonderful!' yelled J. Arnold. 'Such passion! Such feeling! SUCH PINK!'

Just then, a man came in from the set next door. He was a very tall man, dressed in nothing but a little cloth around his waist.

'I say, chaps, has anyone seen my crocodile?' he said. 'Someone seems to have left the door open to the next set and he wandered off.'

'Why, that's Nigel Blatheringthrop!' exclaimed J. Arnold. 'The Jungle Man!'

CHAPTER 20

Homeward Bound

That evening J. Arnold threw a splendid party to celebrate the end of filming. Reggie, Violet and Mynah were guests of honour. There were sugar lumps galore and a huge cake with pink icing and everyone had a marvellous time.

J. Arnold tried to persuade Reggie that he and Violet had a great future in films, but Reggie just smiled and shook his

head. They were all beginning to feel a little tired when Reggie finally asked Mynah to remind J. Arnold that he had made a bargain with them and the time had come for them to go home.

'OK,' sighed J. Arnold. 'I'll put you on an airplane tomorrow.'

'Don't worry, boss,' said Mynah, who had finally got himself into movies with a job as J. Arnold's minder, 'they've got their own transport. C'mon, let's go see them off!' and with that they all piled into big cars and drove down to the sea.

It was a beautiful, moonlit night and the dolphins were waiting for them, playing with the big shell in the shallows. J. Arnold and Alfredo stared in amazement.

Everyone said their goodbyes and Violet gave the two men a big nuzzle with her nose.

'Goodbye, Violet' said J. Arnold. 'You know, it really was a stroke of luck that someone left the door open to the set of that jungle movie. And I'll never know who put out that trail of food leading right up to you. Very lucky!'

Mynah just looked at Reggie and winked. 'Some rhinos have all the luck!' he said.

Violet and Reggie climbed onto the shell. J. Arnold and Alfredo dabbed damp handkerchiefs to their eyes and waved goodbye to the strange little group speeding away over the waves.

'We're going home, Violet!' whispered Reggie as she snuggled up to him on the shell, quite the happiest hippo in the whole wide world.

The End